Edited by Aquila Editing

Proofread by Red Pen Princess

Cover Designer: Mayhem Cover Creations

Hello from Abby!

Thanks for picking up my book! If you want to check out more of my titles, please visit my author page at www.authorabbyknox.com.

While you're there, don't forget to subscribe to my newsletter to keep up with all my latest releases and access free goodies!

Happy reading!

DOCTOR DAVE

ABBY KNOX

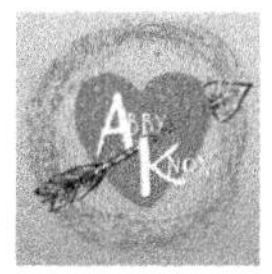

Dedicated to Mr. Abby, who accepted me exactly as I was. Thank you for pushing me without trying to fix me.

Doctor Dave

Working the graveyard shift at a local shopping mall isn't as bad as you think, and 29 year old security guard Millie has plenty of hobbies to help her pass the lonely hours each night. Need a hand-knit animal hat? She's got you covered.

But the best part of her late night job is tuning in to hear bad boy radio personality, Doctor Dave, give out unorthodox dating and sex advice on his live call-in show. With her 30th birthday fast approaching, she's quickly giving up on finding true love for herself. Tonight, however, she's giving it one more chance before taking extreme measures.

Will dialing up the sexy Doctor Dave finally provide the right prescription?

Chapter One

David

It would be reasonable to assume that a radio personality would think to listen to the weather and traffic at the top of the hour before riding his motorcycle to work in December.

But in my case, that would be a wrong assumption.

It's not that I have a death wish. It's that, number one, I love to ride. And number two, a bike makes escaping the local celebrity stalkers in this city a lot easier than an automobile does.

Don't get me wrong; I love my fan base—the honest, non-delusional fan base. I never deny anyone a selfie or an autograph in a safe, public space. But sometimes I get a slightly unhinged super fan waiting around in the parking garage when I finish my show at 2 a.m.

And other times, people like that are waiting to sidle up next to me at one of my speaking gigs or book signings, thinking for some reason that I'd be OK with a stranger's hand sliding into my jeans pocket, looking for…treasure, I guess? Yeah, that happened to me once.

I have in the past perhaps encouraged this kind of behavior by talking too much about my dick on the air. Not in any gross or rated R kind of way—Big Brother FCC is always listening, of course—but my size and girth seem to be popular topics on my show. I don't recall how it started, but it somehow morphed into me having a playboy reputation. Callers lapped it up and advertisers tossed money at the show like nobody's business.

So even though the station manager would prefer I take a taxi to work—a taxi I won't get reimbursed for, by the way. I mean, have you met my station manager? The thrift is strong with this one—I prefer my bike. On my bike, I can maneuver quickly and I'm gone before anybody with bad intentions even notices I've passed by, my helmet adding another handy layer of anonymity.

Even though I'm a six-foot-three, 220 pound man who can bench press his own weight, and most of my super fans are women, I can't be too careful. Never know who's out there watching.

When the shimmers of light freezing rain appear on the sleeves of my leather jacket about a mile from the station tonight, I curse my luck. By the time I reach the underground parking garage, the dancing wisps of icy mist have changed to more of a drizzle. The freezing rain soaks through the thighs of my jeans in no time.

I lock up my bike and, as soon as I'm inside the elevator, I peel off my helmet and leather jacket. I'm soaked through, freezing and disheveled, but my appearance doesn't matter. It's radio, after all. And besides, it's not like I'm going to work to try to impress the woman of my dreams.

No, *The Doctor Dave Show* does not serve to help me find

the woman of my dreams. In fact, the opposite is true: it helps other people find their happily ever after.

The best I can hope for tonight would be a smooth pre-show planning meeting, followed by two hours of solving everyone's relationship dilemmas, and an uneventful ride home to my empty luxury downtown loft.

Honestly, it's all I need for now. After years of treating innumerable STDs at both my private practice and at the free clinic where I volunteer once a week—not to mention counseling thousands of patients and callers about their romantic and sexual drama—most days I feel too jaded to believe a healthy relationship is possible for me. The statistics I've run in my head are pretty bleak when it comes to happily ever afters.

Not that I would ever say that to my callers.

No, they want the snarky, sexy bad boy to empower them to tell their lovers what they want and stop being a pussy, so to speak. They want helpful big brother Dave to urge them to do the things they already know they need to do.

I'm happy to oblige and help them out, but to me the data says, *don't even think about that stuff for yourself, big guy.* So I keep pumping that iron and then go home and pump my own rod. My right hand won't ever give me relationship drama, or chlamydia.

Chapter Two

Millie

I ARRIVE at work a little later than planned, thanks to the freezing rain. The thing is, I'm thankful for the terrible weather because, by being a few minutes late to work, I might narrowly miss seeing Pretzel Guy, as I call him. His actual name escapes me, but the heebie jeebies he gives off never do.

I breathe a sigh of relief when I park my car in the mostly deserted lot at the shopping mall. No sign of Pretzel Guy's windowless van anywhere, *thank goodness.*

Nope, it's just me arriving for work as the last of the mall's cleaning crews are loading up their cars.

Mom calls just as it's time for my shift to start. I'm not excited about stepping out into the freezing rain just yet; in this warmer climate I'm not used to ice. So I take her call as I watch the security lights catch the dance of the freezing rain as it falls and spreads like glitter on the wet asphalt. "Hi, Mom, what's up?" I ask, though I know exactly what's up. It's the same thing that's always up when she calls right before I go in to work my job as a security guard on the graveyard shift at Southfield Mall.

"Jay is going to call you. They need a new receptionist at the construction office. I just want you to know your brothers and I talked about it and we think this would be a good move for you."

My mother raised me and my three very overprotective older brothers by herself since I was 12, and neither she nor my brothers are happy about my line of work. Jay, the oldest, runs his own construction company. The other two, twins Martin and Max, are both cops. My mom, in concert with my brothers, still likes to help me run my life, even though I'm just two years shy of 30.

"I have a job. Plus, Jay isn't going to pay me nearly what I make here."

"Well, it'd just be temporary, anyway, until you find a husband."

"Mom, are you listening to yourself? Did you totally miss the sexual revolution or what?"

She ignores me and keeps going. I get out of my car, lock it up, and head to the security entrance of the mall. I pull up my collar and walk gingerly across the quickly icing-over asphalt so I don't fall flat on my ass.

The controlled indoor climate and the mostly uneventful job waiting for me inside are all things I look forward to. The idea of spending the night alone in a dark shopping mall might scare some people, but I'm what they call an outlier. I like the dark, I like the quiet, and I much prefer them to a bustling mall during the day. I'm not much of a shopper. After all, alone is my general state of being, and sometimes I really like it.

"Who knows, you might meet a nice guy at the construction office," Mom says.

I blurt out a laugh that's a little louder than necessary. "I seriously doubt that," I say, thinking of how many times I've walked past any given construction crew only to be the target of whistles and catcalls. Nice guy, my ass, if that experience is any indication.

"Hey, Millie," drawls a man's voice behind me. Spoke too soon, it seems. "Mom, I'm at work. Gotta go, OK?"

I hang up the phone and turn to Pretzel Guy. "Hey, nasty weather, huh? Anyway, have a good night!"

But despite tiny bits of wet ice catching in his hair, he just stands there, shivering as he stands too close to me while I key in my code for the steel security door. Pretzel Guy and I are semi hidden behind rows of landscaped cypress trees that are just beginning to glaze over with the wet, falling ice. I don't like it when this dude stands so close to me in the dark, hidden from the lights of the parking lot meant to protect people like me.

It's almost like he knows nobody will see us tucked away in this particular spot.

"Late night again?" I try to communicate my disinterest while being polite at the same time. But I swear to god, if he asks me out again, I might not be so polite.

I take solace in the fact that a security camera is trained on the door as I hurriedly work the latch. Meanwhile Pretzel Guy goes on trying to make small talk.

"Rough night for driving," he says, dramatically shivering against the cold, obviously trying to look cute and helpless. Something about his attempts at charm really bother me, but I can't quite put my finger on why.

I shrug and step inside the door, hoping he'll take the hint and skedaddle. "Sure is. Be careful out there. Gotta go!"

I leave him out there in the cold and make sure the door locks behind me. A shiver runs down my back that has nothing to do with the temperature outside.

Soon, the raised hairs on the back of my neck calm down and are replaced by the butterflies in my stomach as I make my way down the hall to the security office where the bank of monitors await my unwavering attention. No, those aren't butterflies in my stomach—more like baby bats.

Jack, the grandfatherly second shift security manager is waiting for me when I clock in. He jangles his keys, anxious to go sooner rather than later in this weather. We exchange pleasantries, then he gives me a heads up on one or two of the cameras that seem to be on the fritz and tells me that the second security guard, Paul, who usually handles the foot patrol and lock checks, won't be coming in tonight.

"Kid is sick with the flu. I tried calling in reinforcements but nobody else wants to come in. Tried calling the maintenance company but nobody wants to come in in this weather. Want me to stay and try to fix the cameras myself? Or..."

He trails off while he continues to jangle his keys, and I know the answer he really wants to hear.

"Nah, go home. Jack. I'm good here. I don't expect I'll be seeing any action tonight. Drive safely, OK?"

He leaves, and I'm actually kind of glad he's not going to be around. I don't want him to witness what's happening tonight.

I unpack my backpack and peel off my winter coat, my uniform already on underneath. Once seated at the bank of monitors, I click on the small radio I keep by the desk and listen to the last hour of the sports talk radio show. I have no idea what they're babbling about but they're funny guys and the voices are decent company. I settle in with the set of needles and luscious, stupid-expensive yarn I brought and resume knitting my current work in progress.

I'm not overly concerned about the wonky camera situation. The general wonkiness has increased lately, but nothing bad has ever happened to me at work because of it. Still, it is annoying. Just another sign that the mall has seen better days when little things fall into disuse and disrepair.

As the clock ticks closer to midnight, the flip-flopping in my stomach grows more intense. And so does a certain delicious anticipation. I can't help but smile as I work through row after row of knitting. What is usually a meditative hobby does nothing to quell my excitement.

So why am I so full of nervous anticipation? Because tonight at midnight, I, Millie Hanson, the unassuming introvert virgin, will be a featured first-time caller on everyone's favorite live romance advice show: The Doctor Dave Show.

Doctor Dave is a bit of a legend in my city, and I've been listening to him for years. That cocky bad boy voice oozes out of my little radio speakers every night at work while I sit at my desk, overseeing all the security monitors deep in the bowels of the mall offices.

A few months ago, I emailed the show's producer to tell her my story in hopes of speaking to Doctor Dave on the show. And what do you know? They picked me. Turns out live radio is more orchestrated than I realized, and they scheduled me to call in tonight.

I only hope my mother and brothers don't listen because this is potentially very embarrassing.

At five minutes to midnight, I make the call. My fingers shake as I punch in the number on the desk phone. I would use my personal cell phone to call in, but the producer said a landline, if available, is preferred for sound quality and reliability. So, if corporate spies are listening in on the mall's phone lines, they are in for an earful tonight. But they probably aren't listening. Hell, they can't be bothered to fix a couple of cameras, so why would they be listening to phone conversations?

I take a sip of my tea to fight off dry mouth, and then set my knitting down in my lap. I'm not even going to attempt to continue knitting while I speak to the dashing hunk of manhood who will soon pick up on the other end of the line, but I feel the need to keep the soft yarn handy. Always good to have something soft and cozy to hang on to.

Once connected, Reagan, the show's producer, instructs me to turn down my radio, and adds, "Don't ask the doctor any personal questions. And don't try to ask him out or give him your personal number." She sounds a bit territorial, but I shake it off, realizing that with his bad boy reputation and his amazing voice, women probably throw themselves at him all the time. I've heard stories about female listeners sending him their panties in the mail. Hell, even on the show he and Reagan have joked about women actually showing up to the studio like groupies, trying to get alone time with him.

As I wait to be connected live on the air with Doctor Dave, I try to steady my breathing, but it's a losing battle.

I text my best friend Jenny: *Oh god, am I really doing this?*

Her answer is an immediate: *YES*.

I type: *Is he going to be able to tell I have the world's most massive crush on him?* I inhale deeply and exhale slowly to calm my galloping heart rate. I don't imagine a caller having a cardiac episode on the air would be great for his ratings.

Jenny replies: *Every caller has a crush on him. That's kind of the deal. Just go with it.*

When Jenny and I went out for drinks and decided to make a list of surmountable things that scare us, I should have said I wanted to learn how to ride a horse or surf.

When Jenny told me to do one thing every day that scares me, did she mean this? My memory is fuzzy from too much tequila that night. Did she mean a little scary? Or something that fills me with abject terror? Because that's what I feel right now as I wait for Doctor Dave to come on the line.

I hear the click on the phone, and feel as though I've inhaled all the air out of the room.

"Millie. You're on the air. Talk to me, baby." Doctor Dave's voice nuzzles my ear. I feel tingles everywhere.

My heart no longer gallops. I think it actually stops for a second.

I can't breathe, I can't speak.

Fuck. I'm going to fuck this up, live on the radio.

"Millie, sweetheart, are you there?"

Oh my god, did he just…? *Get a hold of yourself, Millie.* He calls every female caller sweetheart. He gives everyone pet names, irrespective of gender. That's his shtick. He makes everyone feel special in order to put them at ease before delivering the advice that some people sometimes don't want to hear.

I open my mouth but no words come out. I'm going to blow it. I expect him to give up and stop wasting precious airtime on me, and maybe that's exactly what should happen. I've lost my nerve, I've lost my chance, and maybe I've dodged a bullet. Maybe my sudden muteness is a blessing from the universe, preventing me from suffering humiliation on a live radio show broadcast out to the entire city.

But then something magical happens in my ear. Doctor Dave drops his voice lower, softer, like he's right there, murmuring into my ear. He presses me. "Millie, honey. I can hear you breathing. I know you're there." The sound of his gentle chuckle produces a delicious clenching between my thighs. He continues. "Is this an obscene phone call? Because I gotta be honest. It's working for me, baby."

The naughty doctor's words bust through some barrier inside me and I laugh in both amusement and relief.

"I'm…I'm here. Hi. Hello." The words all come out more breathy than intended but I'm elated that I'm at least no longer voiceless.

"Thank god, because the next caller's yet another sad sack dude just waiting for me to tell him what he doesn't want to hear."

"You mean 'man up'?" I say, assuming his producer will add everyone's favorite "man up" sound drop, and I have to roll my eyes. The sound drops and the catch-phrases are the only thing I can't stand about the show, and I've always sensed that Doctor Dave himself loathes them, too.

"That's probably the long and short of it, no pun intended. You, on the other hand, have an incredibly sexy voice and I happen to really, really like that name. Millie. I'd much rather start the show with a bang. Pun intended."

I giggle like an idiot, but this only eggs him on.

"I mean it, it's cute. You've got to be cute with a name like Millie, right? You know you're cute, don't you?"

I swallow the saliva in my mouth and realize my salivary glands are not the only part of me that's dripping. How in the hell does he do that?

"I…I guess so? I mean, I'm not uncute," I reply. I

smack my palm to my forehead. *Uncute is not even a word, you moron!*

"OK, OK, my producer is giving me the mom look right now so we'd better get to the meat of your problem. Don't want a spanking from Mama tonight. How can Doctor Dave help you tonight, sweet Millie?"

Swallowing again, I kick shy, stammering, quivering Millie to the curb and get to the point.

"Well, I'm twenty-eight years old and still a virgin, and I no longer wish to be one. Problem is, I can't seem to find the right guy for the job."

Doctor Dave pauses for a moment.

"Virginity is so relative. A lot of people do lots of sexy things and still consider themselves to be virgins."

I smile and say to him indulgently, "Yes, I know that, Doctor Dave. I've been listening to you for five years. I assure you I am as pure as the driven snow."

He makes a strange, throaty noise, and I can't tell whether it's approving or disapproving. "Obviously we're talking about penile/vaginal intercourse. What about digital penetration?"

I sigh and swallow nervously. This is really putting myself out there. I hope nobody recognizes my voice. "How about I tell you what I *have* done? It's a much shorter list."

He chuckles good-naturedly. "All right, baby, give it to me."

Oh god, this flirty talk. I have to remind myself it's not real. It's only for the radio. But his advice is real enough, so I keep going.

"I held hands with Jerry Pulaski in the fourth grade during the couple skate."

Long pause.

"I'm sorry, *couple skate*?" he asks.

I explain, "Yes. At the roller rink. They played 'Waterfalls' by TLC and called 'couple skate' and we skated together for the whole song and then when it was over, he didn't say anything and I didn't say anything. And we both went and sat with our friends and ate popcorn, and that was it."

I chew on my lip and wait for him to reply, my feelings punching at the walls of my throat.

Chapter Three

David

I scrape the stubble on my chin thoughtfully. "And that's it?" I ask her.

She pauses, and I smile. This is the kind of caller who reminds me why I do this job. Lately, I'm getting tired of the same problems. Same sound drops. Same catchphrases. Every night feels like the movie *Groundhog Day*, except in my version, there's no amazing woman at the end waiting for me to stop fucking shit up.

This caller might just be the end to my Groundhog Day. This caller might even be worth my bike sliding home in the freezing rain after the show. I feel no pain when she talks.

"Well," Millie stammers. "I kissed a boy I had a crush on during a game of spin the bottle in high school. But it was just a peck, and the guy was my friend anyway. He came out a week later as gay, and he assured me that I didn't have anything to do with him being gay because at the time I didn't know it doesn't work like that."

Normally, I don't like it when callers ramble on, but something about her voice gets to me. I immediately like her. Her sweetness comes through in her shaky inhales and her soft drawl. But it's not simply a saccharine surface. Lots of people seem sweet, but are just waiting for the right moment to strike with their venom. Millie, on the other hand, doesn't hide anything malicious beneath what she shows to the world, and I have been doing this long enough to read people. Millie is—there's no other word for it—pure.

"So you're telling me there's been no real kissing? No tongue kissing at all…with anyone?"

"Correct."

The feeling of protectiveness rising up in my chest continues to grow. Now I'm conflicted about making good radio versus protecting her from revealing too much about her sex life to hundreds of thousands of listeners.

So I switch gears. "Millie, what do you do?"

"Couple of things. I work as a security guard, and I knit."

"Knitting? What do you knit?"

"I knit animal earmuffs and hats and I sell them on the internet. I do pretty well with it, actually. I'm…I'm working on one set right now."

"Animal earmuffs. Things that look like animals for kids to wear?"

Her shy, breathy laugh hits me somewhere in my chest and squeezes me. "Not exactly. I knit things for young farm animals to wear in cold weather."

If I wasn't paying attention before…

"Wait a minute, back up. You knit little tiny hats and

earmuffs for baby animals to wear? Enlighten me some more."

"Well, sometimes farmers want warm ear coverings for calves, baby goats, donkeys, whatever animals they have. I promise it's a real thing. Google it."

"Llamas?"

"I have done some for baby llamas and alpacas, yes," she says with an indulging smile in her voice.

"You're telling me your name is Millie and you make little bitty hats for baby farm animals, *and* you're a virgin?"

"Ye—yes?"

I have to stop myself from blurting something out. Something like an immediate marriage proposal. It's too much to process how fucking cute she is. And she's not even my type! She's too shy for me.

"I'm sorry. I'm having trouble processing these feelings I'm having right now," I say.

A small gasp from her lands in my ears. "Uhm, why?"

I clear my throat, and through the window of the sound booth, my producer Reagan gives me a grossed-out look. I'm so rattled I forgot to use the cough button.

"So. No boyfriend, not dating anyone currently. That's good."

"Excuse me?" she squeaks.

"Sorry. That's not what I meant." That's a lie. That's absolutely what I meant. The idea of this sweet, pure woman on a date with anybody but me makes my blood pressure rise. This is insane; I've taken thousands of calls from women over the years, all of them sexy in their own way, but not a single one of them has made me feel things down in my guts.

Reagan is looking at me with both excitement and bewilderment, probably because to her, it sounds like I'm on the verge of hitting on a caller—not just flirting.

I'm flustered. Goddamn it. Smooth talking Doctor Dave the radio personality does not get flustered. David Hart, M.D. can discuss all manner of gross situations and injuries in a dignified manner. Plain old David Hart, single guy, on the other hand, is absolutely unsettled, and he is fucking this all right up.

I could continue to play off what I've just said for the sake of professional radio and to hide my feelings. I could do that. But something inside me doesn't want to play it cool.

"Actually, that's exactly what I meant. I like you, and I'm feeling a little bit protective," I say.

She replies, "Can I be honest with you, Doctor Dave?"

"God, yes, please."

"My three older brothers have been overly protective of me my entire life, and they're part of the problem. They've been scaring boys away from me since I was fourteen."

I have to chuckle. "I like them already."

Millie's tone turns slightly indignant. "Well, I don't need another caveman brother," she says. "I need you—I mean, I need someone objective to tell me how to find the right candidate to have sex with me."

Sign me up. *I volunteer as tribute*, I want to say.

I take a sip of water to counteract my dry mouth and to cool off the fire she's stoking inside me.

"Describe the right candidate," I reply.

"Well, I don't necessarily want a relationship. But I'm open to it if one develops naturally. Whether or not it is a one-night stand, the guy doesn't have to be perfect. I don't care about washboard abs—I mean, I'm not exactly a petite girl myself. But I do want him to be kind and patient, and confident enough to do me this favor. Plus, well, he should be fun to talk to, you know, before and after."

I can practically hear her blushing when she says "before and after." It's so freaking adorable.

These feelings in my chest, my stomach, and now in my pants, keep sending the same irrational thought to my brain. That thought is: *me*. It needs to be me. I can already picture this amazing woman in my head, I understand completely what she wants, and there can be nobody else —nobody but me—to help her navigate her first time. I'm the only one who can treat her right. I know exactly how to make her feel sexy. How to build her up, get her ready, please her, and blow her mind. How to usher her to a fucking incredible orgasm, and then take excellent care of her afterward.

It absolutely has to be me.

No other choice exists. She's mine.

"Has anybody tried?"

"Well, there is a guy where I work that sometimes asks me out, but I'm really not interested," she says.

If she could see the way my nostrils flare with jealously and rage, it might scare the hell out of her.

"And you haven't given that guy the boot yet? What's his name?"

She laughs. "Honestly, I call him Pretzel Guy in my head because I can't remember his name. He manages the soft pretzel kiosk at the mall where I work."

"Wait," I say, my alarm bells going off in my head. "You said you work the overnight shift. What the hell is Pretzel Guy still doing there while you're at work?"

Millie attempts to explain the situation, clearly feeling bad about mentioning Pretzel Guy on the air. "Oh, well, he works late, I guess. He says he has to stay late to knead the dough and get things ready for the morning. I think. He's usually on his way out when I'm on my way in, but he always has to stop and say hi to me. I mean, maybe I'm wrong and he's just trying to be friendly—"

"No. Nope," I interject. "Trust your gut on this one, Millie. That guy is bad news. I want you to stop being nice to him immediately. That's the only language guys like that understand. The next time you see him, tell him you have a boyfriend and he doesn't like other guys sniffing around his girl."

"But I don't have a boyfriend."

"You will soon enough," I say. What am I saying? I can't promise this woman something like that.

Oh, my conscience tells me, *but can't you?*

"Shouldn't a simple rejection be enough for a guy to back off? Why should I have to lie about having a boyfriend?"

"You're absolutely right. Sorry, my testosterone took over. You keep having this effect on me, Millie."

Reagan's mouth drops open and she's fanning herself and giving me the thumbs up. My producer seems to think this whole thing I'm doing with Millie is a bit. It isn't. But Reagan doesn't need to know that, yet.

This might indeed be good radio but the truth is, I'm thinking of this lonely, sweet, sexy virgin alone in a shopping mall at night, as she describes some guy who can't take no for an answer, and all sorts of things are happening to my body. I'm hot. My muscles are tight like I'm ready to street fight, and…yep, there it is…my cock is jerking awake.

In all my years of doing this radio gig and flirting with countless women—all of whom I truly cared about and did my best to help—never have any of them evoked a physical reaction like this from me.

Millie's laughter sends a tingle down my back. "OK, it's not like he's going to kidnap me or something."

"Trust me, Millie. He's already lied to you. That ain't a French patisserie he's running. They get that cheap-ass dough out of the freezer in the morning and boom. Done."

"What's a patisserie?"

I seem to be on a roll with blurting out the first thing that pops into my head, so here comes another one. "A type of French bakery. Someday we'll go to Paris together and eat croissants until we're ready to burst."

Millie goes quiet for a moment. My eyes snap up to Reagan, who is holding up her hands and mouthing the words, "What the fuck?" I can read her face; she thinks the bit is going too far.

My Millie saves the day by playing off what I've said like it's superficial flirting. "Sure, let's go right now," she replies with the cutest, sexiest laugh I've ever heard.

I give her my deepest signature Doctor Dave sexy chuckle. "Just you and me, baby."

Millie makes a noise that almost sounds dismissive. "You know what I think?"

"Yes, I do. I think I know exactly what you're thinking, sweetheart."

But she's not responding to my schtick anymore. "I think there's something more to you than this womanizing playboy persona you have on the radio. Am I right about that?"

Suddenly, she's not laughing anymore, or volleying any more sexy banter.

Struggling to right this crashing aircraft, I pull up. "Who says I'm a womanizer? And a playboy?"

"Everyone. Literally everyone. In fact, I'm looking at the station website right now and those words are in your bio."

Mental note: Change my bio. And then throttle whoever wrote that garbage.

"Millie. I can't tell you why right now. But it's important to me that you understand I am not a lothario. I love and respect women."

"I know," she says. The smile in her voice has returned. My breathing calms. What kind of a ride is she taking me on here? "I've listened to you for years and I've read all your books. You might be a major flirt on the air but your advice is sound, you treat everyone with kindness, and you're pretty funny, too."

Coming from some people, her words might sound like hero worship, which I've never cared for. But from her, it feels as necessary as water. It's not my ego that feels good when she says stuff like that, but some other part of me that wants to make her feel as special as she makes me feel.

"Well, let's not get carried away. I'm not that awesome. Back to you. Tell me about your dating experiences."

"Well, like I said, my three older brothers pretty much scared off any guys who came sniffing around. My dad was a pastor but left the family when I was a teenager. He wasn't the best example of how a man should treat a woman. He wasn't abusive or anything, but always had a comment about my clothes or what I ate or the way I talked. Nothing I said or did was *ladylike* enough for him. After he left my mom for his church secretary, I guess I rebelled by eating things he never allowed me to eat. I never slept around because I guess the fear he'd instilled in me kinda stuck."

I'm shaking my head and trying not to crack my knuckles in response to all of this. "First of all, you're a human being. You are built to eat good food and have good sex. Our bodies are designed for these things to bring us pleasure and a little bit of happiness in this fucked up world. Oh god. Sorry."

Reagan is freaking out in the sound booth, but she's got a hair trigger response for that dump button.

Millie gasps and laughs, but I reassure her that's what the seven-second delay is for.

"But I probably shouldn't let that happen again or the station manager will be on my ass."

Millie laughs again, and it's different from the nervous, breathy Millie from a few minutes ago. It's high and tumbles through the line like the sounds of a wind chime. She empowers me to continue. My listeners for some reason love it when I talk shit about the boss. "Actually, no, he won't be on my ass because he's at home asleep on his overpriced mattress, a gift from one of the advertisers that my show brought in, thank you very much. Did I get a fancy mattress? No, I just get chewed out every night by him for speaking the truth."

She continues to laugh. I'm so proud I could thump my chest like a gorilla. *Alpha male cause female to make happy sound.*

I don't thump my chest. Instead I turn the focus back on to Millie. "Tell me about some of the dates you've been on."

She takes a deep breath.

I can already tell I'm not going to like what she has to say.

Chapter Four

Millie

"THE TRUTH IS, I'm surprisingly boy crazy for someone so shy," I tell him. "I've been set up on plenty of blind dates with guys who I thought were very attractive. But it never ends well. One of them asked me how long I was going to stay with my dead-end job, not even bothering to ask me if I actually enjoy my so-called dead-end job. Another time, someone set me up with a doctor and I thought we were getting along. Then he told me what I think is actually a clue as to why I rarely get asked on second dates—he said my boobs were too big. So, I'm open to having breast reduction surgery, because I wonder if that might boost my confidence when I'm on a date. What do you think?"

"Do they cause you any medical problems? Back pain, et cetera?"

"No."

"Well then, he's an idiot. You're perfect the way you are."

I blush so deeply I'm thankful that Dr. Dave can't see me right now.

"Dr. Dave, you can't see them. They really are too big."

"I can assure you that's not a thing unless they cause you discomfort. He's a dipshit."

I gasp and laugh out loud.

"Apologies for the language. Reagan. You're not sleeping on the seven-second-delay button, are ya?"

I continue to giggle. Oh my god, I haven't laughed this much in so long. I feel like something inside me is unclenching. Relaxing. His voice is even more rough and sexy over the phone than it is on the radio and my body—which doesn't understand that it's all just innocent flirting—responds to it. My heart races; my nipples feel tight and every nerve ending between my thighs crackles. Beyond that, my emotions are becoming unruly. If I'm not careful, I'm going to develop more than a crush on this voice on the other end of the line. Real feelings could start to elbow their way in.

"I'm going to stop you right there, though. What's your cup size?"

This question does not shock me. While Dr. Dave is a professional, he doesn't shy away from his playboy persona on the air. He peppers his advice with plenty of mild flirting. It's that combination of professional advice giver and shock jock that makes me enjoy listening to him so much.

And now that I'm actually on the phone with him? Maybe my enjoyment is crossing the line into a serious yet unrequited infatuation.

"I'm not sure," I say, embarrassed. "All I know is nothing fits. The witches at the lingerie store here at the mall—you know the one—have made it perfectly clear that they don't carry anything that fits me."

"First thing you need to do is be properly fitted. I have a cloth measuring tape. I'll do it myself if you come down to the studio," he offers. It's true. He's done this kind of stunt on the radio before. I remember one time, he had a bit where he guessed listeners' cup sizes and then had them measured by a staff member to see if he was correct.

I reply, "I would but I can't leave the mall."

He's quiet for a moment. "You have department stores at that mall?"

"Yes, I do."

"Do you have a key? Go down there right now and get a tape measure; I'm sure they have some in the lingerie department."

"I'm definitely not going to do that."

"OK. Sorry. Did I come off too strong?"

I sigh. What is he playing at? Do I care? My quickly dampening undies right now do not care. "I don't feel objectified; I just can't go rifling through their things. I'll get caught on camera and be fired by morning."

Dr. Dave tries again. "You know what? Forget about getting fitted for now. Send me a picture of yourself and I'll tell you your cup size. And I promise it's not too big by anybody's reasonable standards."

"You want me to send a photo of myself?"

"When we go to commercial, I'll give you the email address where you can send it right to my desk here in the booth."

I bite my lip. This is strange but…well…he is a doctor.

"OK, I'm working on the photo right now," I say.

I put the desk phone on speaker so I can keep listening to Dr. Dave while I unbutton my uniform shirt.

"Working on it? OK, do what you gotta do, angel," he says, sounding a little bit confused.

"Almost ready," I say.

He moves on to the subject of my abysmal dating life. "While I'm waiting on that photo, Millie, let's forget about all those wrong guys you've dated. The only thing you need to boost your confidence is you. I'm pretty good at reading people and I already know you are smart, kind, thoughtful, funny, beautiful. You just have to believe that about yourself."

The sound of his voice, and his words, makes my skin react with goosebumps as I bare my flesh. I remove my bra and quickly take the photo. It's dim, but you can still see everything in the light coming from the security monitors in front of me. That should be enough to get his opinion.

I hear him say, "And that's a commercial break. You still there, Millie?"

"I'm here."

His voice is slightly different. More earnest. "I'm dead serious. I think the only thing wrong with you is that you've been picking the wrong guys. Thank your lucky stars you're still a virgin."

I pick the phone back up and take him off speaker, even though I'm still not finished buttoning myself back up.

"If you say so, I guess."

"Millie," he says. "I want you to stay on the line and I want to keep talking, is that all right? I think we have a lot to talk about, you and I."

The way he says "you and I" makes me shiver.

As my hands brush against the skin on my chest, I feel my nipples tighten some more. "I'm good with that. I'd like to keep talking to you, too."

"Good. I like your voice—hope that doesn't creep you out," he says.

I bite my lip. "Thank you. No, you don't creep me out. If you did, I would never have called. I don't know how to find the right guy, but I for sure know which guys are the wrong ones."

He pauses slightly. "And how do you think you'll know when you've met the right one?"

"Well, I don't know exactly how I'll know. But I think he would have to be … well … be more like you."

Chapter Five

David

CHECKING MY EMAIL, I see that Millie's message with her photo has arrived. Dying of curiosity, I click on it.

Oh. Shit.

That's a selfie all right. A topless selfie showing her from the neck all the way down to her navel.

For what must be the first time in my entire broadcast career, I fumble my words.

"Dr. Dave? You still there?"

Am I here? No, I'm floating somewhere above the clouds.

There she is. Tendrils of light brown hair haphazardly fall around bare shoulders, framing her exquisite rack. The lighting is dim but I can see everything. Her abundant breasts are as she described: large, yes, but nothing I can't handle, with erect, dusky nipples begging me to warm them up.

She's so fucking beautiful.

And I am in so much trouble if anyone sees this.

I have two choices right now: Tell her that's not what I asked for and explain that I meant a photo of herself dressed. Or simply say thank you and give her my guess as to her cup size.

It seems irrelevant now. Even without a second glance I know she's a Triple E cup.

Of course I email back my only choice: *Thank you. Triple E, love. We're back on the air in a few seconds, and we don't have to talk about cup size anymore.*

I delete her email. What I'm not going to do is allow anyone else to see this photo and use it for a bit. I'm not going to let my producer Reagan make it part of the show, nor anyone else.

"Beautiful," I say over the phone. "Just beautiful."

She pauses for a second and replies, "Thank you."

"Send me a picture of just your face…"

"Dr. Dave, we're on the air!" shouts Reagan from the producer's booth.

"Oh crap, how much of that went live?"

She leans into the microphone and laughs, "Enough. But do keep flirting with the caller, I want to hear more."

I refresh the email at my desk, eager for the photo of her face to appear while I keep talking. "You know, Millie, you come off as shy at first, but you've got a very brave heart. Listeners, don't underestimate shy people. Sometimes they can shock you to your core…"

The photo of Millie's face arrives and I click on it so fucking hard. There's a cute, messy bun. Luminous skin. Her full lips, parted in half a smile, match the color of her nipples that are now forever branded in my memory. Wit and innocence sparkle in her eyes. There is something so sweet and vulnerable about what she did. She's so open hearted, I can't understand why someone hasn't snatched her up.

"Clearly, there is nothing wrong with you. All these men are imbeciles. You should come to one of my speaking events. I'd love to meet up with you. I can get you a VIP ticket."

"You don't have to do that. Besides, I've seen you before. I worked security last time you did a charity thing where I work," she says.

I remember that event. Southfield Mall. It was a fundraiser for childhood cancer research. I don't say it out loud on the air. First of all, I don't want listeners to know where she works and also I don't want to toot my own horn.

"Those events are full of admirers and super fans waiting in lines ten miles long. You have me on the phone now. What are you waiting for?" Millie says.

I glance up at Reagan. Her eyebrows are raised and she does a hand signal for me to keep going.

Chapter Six

Millie

NOTHING about this conversation is going the way I thought it would.

My feelings are all over the place.

What began as an innocent crush has turned into something else. Full-blown real-life affection. This isn't a fantasy anymore and if he's toying with me, so help me god, I will swallow my pride and sic my biggest brother on him faster than you can say "soft pretzel with hot melted industrial cheese product."

And that would not end well. My middle brother, Max, is bigger than all of them. And not only is he a cop, but also a locally famous, semi-professional wrestler in his spare time. Max would not hesitate to put Doctor Dave in the ground with one word from me.

Treading carefully, my voice trembling more than I wish it would, I say, "So, do you have any advice for me? About…my problem?"

The way he's breathing through his nose sounds like an angry bull. I wonder if people listening over the airwaves can hear it.

I check the time and it's 12:30 a.m. already. Time to do the walkabout and check on all the locks. I never thought this phone call would go on so long. We've only taken one commercial break when I'm pretty sure there should have been three. And he should be on his third caller by now. I know from listening that the station manager and his advertisers are going to be livid by now.

"I do. I do have advice for you, Millie." The sexy, gravelly sound of his voice ricochets inside my abdomen, building up a craving so intense it hurts. I try to take a deep breath to keep my hands from shaking but it only stimulates the lump in my throat, triggering tears in the corners of my eyes from the sheer emotional tension.

I can't control the hoarse whisper that escapes me, knowing it's going to be unintelligible on the radio. "What? What's your advice? I'm dying over here."

Almost before I can finish that sentence, he blurts out, "It's me. I want to be the one. Wait for me."

All the air puffs out of my lungs and a tear spills down my cheek. "No. This can't be real. You did not just tell me to save my virginity for you."

"Yes, I fucking did."

I don't even care that he's cussing on the air. I'm way more concerned that he might be playing with me. But he's not. I called him on it, and I think he's telling the truth.

"I...I...I don't know how to respond to that."

"Listen. Stay on the line. I don't want to go but they're forcing me to take another call. But stay on the line and make sure Reagan has your number just in case we drop you. I need to talk to you off the air. OK, sweetheart?"

Of all the times I've heard that famous voice say "sweetheart," this is the first time I've felt as if it's sincere.

I swallow and wipe a tear off my cheek. "OK," I breathe. "I'll be right here. I'm not going anywhere."

"See that you don't, baby."

He clicks me on hold, and I wait while need slicks my undies and emotions slither through my gut and squeeze my stomach like a boa constrictor.

Chapter Seven

David

"REAGAN, where the fuck did she go?"

She shrugs, looking disinterested in my distress over her dropping Millie off the line.

"Get me the number!" I bellow.

"Dave, you're back on the air in three minutes, and you're in the middle of another call."

"I'm going to ignore the fact that you're pretending to be my handler right now and ask again nicely. Give me her number."

She sighs. "I don't have her number. She was a scheduled call-in."

I grit out, "Check the caller ID logs. I told her to stay on the line, so I need to call her back."

Reagan stands up. "If I do this for you, will you get back in there and get ready to come back from commercial?"

She digs out the number from our call logs and I type it into my cell phone and click call.

She doesn't answer.

Shit. Shit, shit, shit. Where the fuck is she?

I know she's not sitting at her security desk ignoring me. Or is she?

No. No, I don't think that's right.

I pace around the studio, but I don't prepare to go back on the air. Instead I check my computer's email for the message she sent earlier with the photo of her face. Jackpot. At the end of her email is her automatic signature. Millie Hansen, her knitted animal accessories website link, some random quote about big-breasted girls, and her cell phone number.

I punch it into my personal cell phone and hit the call button.

And I wait.

Chapter Eight

Millie

"Where did you go?"

I'm still trying to process the fact that Dr. Dave is calling me on my cell phone. How is this happening? I mean, I'm glad it's happening. I'm elated it's happening. I now feel pretty sure this is not part of a long joke being played on me by his radio persona. This is real. He sought out my number and is sounding pretty peeved that my call got dropped.

"I don't know. I was waiting, like you said. Then the call got dropped by accident, I guess. And in the meantime I had to leave my desk to do the lock checks. Normally, it's not my job, but Paul's kid is sick…well, you don't want to hear about that. So now I'm doing that. You know, walking around to make sure everything is locked up and there's no shenanigans going on late at night at the mall."

I could be mistaken, but the noise he makes on the

other end almost sounds like an angry caveman grunt. Even more shocking is that my body kind of likes it.

"I don't like the idea of you walking around the dark mall alone late at night, Millie."

"Trust me, nothing ever happens here. Unless you count the occasional rat rooting around the soft pretzel stand. I don't think Pretzel Guy cleans it up very well at night."

Dr. Dave mutters something about not wanting to talk about Pretzel Guy anymore.

"Hey," I interject. "Aren't you supposed to be on the air with another caller right now?"

"Yeah, in about another minute."

My heart drops. "Oh. Well, do you want me to go?"

"No," he growls. "Don't fucking go anywhere. If the call gets dropped, find the best reception and I'll call you back. OK? I don't want to waste another second. Listen, where are you right now?"

I glance around and say, "I'm standing in front of that lingerie store. You know, the one with the fashion show with the angel wings…"

He grunts. "I'm familiar. Fuck. Now I'm picturing those gorgeous, lickable breasts of yours in something from that store."

I laugh. "Good luck with that. They don't carry my cup size, remember? I've never been able to shop at that store. It's so depressing."

Dr. Dave cusses, berating himself for making me feel bad.

"It's fine," I say.

I hear him breathing while he pauses. "Let's have some fun, baby. What do you say?"

I bite my lip, wishing he could see the grin he's provoking on my face. "What did you have in mind?"

He cuts to the chase. "Millie. This is crazy and it may be hard for you to believe, but this connection is real. I feel it. Are you feeling it?"

I suck in a breath and have to cover my mouth to keep from smiling like an even bigger idiot. But why? Nobody is here to see it.

"Yes, I do feel it," I whisper, my hand going to my chest, as if my heart might burst out of it at any minute.

"Baby, listen. This show is over in an hour. Then I'm coming to where you are and we are going to do exactly what you said."

Sparks ignite and crackle over every inch of my skin. Is this really happening? "Are you saying you really want to be my first?"

"I thought that was painfully obvious. I've been telling you this."

"I thought it was just good radio."

"Baby, you're not just good radio. You're good everything."

I am full-on white-knuckle gripping the glass railing around the second floor right now because my knees are about to buckle. How am I so powerless against his charms?

Somebody is pounding on something and I realize the sound is coming from his phone. "What's that?"

"It's my producer. I locked myself in the bathroom so I can talk to you, and so she'll have no choice but to run another couple of commercials."

"Oh gosh. I don't want you to get into trouble," I tell him.

"I'm already in trouble, in more ways than one. Now what do you say? Let me come pick you up and we'll…talk about how and where you'd like to do this. If you want me to. Do you want me to?"

I sigh a shivering sigh. "I would love to, but you're forgetting something. I'm at work here until seven."

"Sweetheart, you can just quit that job. You're with me, now."

Well, that was not what I was expecting. I feel the need to set him straight. "Listen. I like my job. I like my independence. I like my life. I don't need you to whisk me away, OK?"

"OK. Fair enough. Sorry. I got overwhelmed and I'm really eager to see you, angel."

He's called me every pet name in the book over the last thirty minutes and it never gets old. The tingles just keep coming.

"Well, in the entire scope of things, a few hours isn't that long of a wait, is it?"

He laughs. "Gonna be the longest few hours of my fucking life."

"Well, I can give you something to think about in the meantime," I say, hardly believing the weird fantasy I'm about to reveal.

Doctor Dave groans. "Oh, baby, don't tell me. No, wait. Yes, tell me."

I close my eyes and cringe as I say it. "You know those big linen stores that sell all the bedroom and bathroom stuff? They have one here. Well, I have a weird secret. Do you want to hear it?"

"You're killing me, doll. And, abso-fucking-lutely I do." The low register of his voice continues to violate me through the phone. And I find it delicious.

I continue. "Well, I've always had a little fantasy about hooking up with a nameless, faceless guy at the linen store. You know, on one of those really tastefully decorated bedding displays?"

He pauses, and I'm ready to feel humiliated if he laughs at my silly fantasy.

"You mean those little half-size beds with a thousand throw pillows that are not actually meant for sleeping?"

"Yeah," I say, waiting for the ax to fall.

Instead I hear a low, guttural growl and the word "fuck." And then he says, "I can't let you have a nameless hookup on one of those stupid mini beds. Millie, that's gonna be me on that bed with you."

"Oh, OK." I can barely get out the words, I'm so happy.

More pounding and shouting.

I think Dr. Dave is in more trouble at work than he's letting on.

"Where are you, precisely?"

I let him know that now, I'm right in front of the sporting goods store.

"Are you anywhere where the security cameras can see you?"

I grin. "It just so happens I'm in a dead zone. The cameras in this area have been acting wonky for a while now."

His voice drops lower and he whispers, "Find a secluded spot right now. I want you to get ready for me."

Shaking all over, I duck into a nook by the maintenance access doors, in between the hippie crystals store and the one that sells all the pop culture tee-shirts. "Done," I breathe.

"Now, I don't want to freak you out but—"

"Do it. Be freaky."

His words sweep over my skin like feathers. "Put your sweet hand down your panties."

As if I hadn't thought of that. I unzip my pants and slip my hand down the front of my panties. "Done."

"Are you wet?"

I slide my hand deeper. "God, yes," I breathe. "The way you talk to me? I don't have to touch myself to know I'm wet."

"Fuck," he whispers.

I close my eyes as my fingers sweep down the bare skin of my bikini area, farther down toward my split. My whole body is electrified, anticipating what he might tell me to do next.

"I'm so fucking hard for you right now, baby. Rub yourself while I talk to you," he says. "And close your eyes."

My hand slides lower, rubbing, while my fingers slip in between my folds. The wetness is unreal, and the sensation of my hand's exploration and Dr. Dave's voice in my ear drenches me even more.

"When you scream my name, I want you to call me David. OK? That's my name. Dave is the guy on the radio. Me, here, with you, I'm just David. OK?"

"OK. Tell me what you want me to do next," I plead.

"Has my sweet virgin ever gotten herself off before?"

I'm so hot right now my eyes want to roll back in my head and I fear my knees might give out. But I keep control of myself and answer him. "Yes."

"Touch your clit and tell me what it feels like."

When my fingers swipe my tight button, my body jerks and I let out a small whimper before biting down on my lip. My cheeks feel hot. "Oh!"

"What does it feel like?"

I squeeze it gently. "Hard. A little achy and throbbing. It wants you, not me."

"Sweetheart, you are letting me get away with murder, you know that?"

My words sound like the sins I've yet to commit when I

reply, "David, you could get away with anything at all when it comes to me."

Chapter Nine

David

My hand squeezes my cock but the sensation of my own hand is nothing compared to the shivers of pleasure her voice gives me. "Fucking hell, that's some filthy talk coming from a baby-animal-hat knitting virgin named Millie."

She sighs, and I can tell she's not lying. She is most definitely touching herself while we talk. "You bring it out in me," she breathes.

Reagan pounds on the door.

"Dave, what the fuck!"

I cover the phone mic with a finger from my free hand. "Run a house ad! Jesus!"

My producer is pissed. "We already ran like seven house ads, the station manager is getting calls from angry listeners. Calls at home, Dave! Come on!"

I shake my head. I know that most of my listeners are normal, sane people. But you can't be too careful. How do some of these psychopaths find out the home phone number of the station manager? This is why I don't use my last name on the air. I grit my teeth as I realize I should start a new policy of all my callers using fake names. I don't want people like Millie targeted by some deranged lunatic.

The arousing thoughts of my Millie touching herself while my voice is in her ear is now competing with Reagan's angry voice, which is bringing me back to reality. I can't slap one out in the bathroom at work. What the hell am I thinking?

But at the same time I can't let her hang up.

"Millie, sweetheart, I have to go. Dammit, I don't want to leave you hanging like this but…just promise me you'll stay on the line, OK?"

She gasps in a breath and lets out a shuddering sigh. "Uhm, I'm not going anywhere, doctor."

"David," I remind her. "I'm your guy, Millie. You call me David."

Chapter Ten

David

THE NEXT THING I hear is her breath catching in surprise, and it's not because I've turned her on.

"Millie, sweetheart, what is it?"

"Huh," she says. "That's weird."

I don't like the sound of this.

"Tell me what's weird."

"Somebody left a light on at the sporting goods store, way in the back. I just noticed. I don't remember it being on before."

"Don't go over there," I insist.

She protests. "But it's my job. I have to check it out. It'll be fine."

"Millie, get out of there now. I don't like this, I don't like this at all," I say urgently.

"It's fine I'm just gonna go turn the…" She trails off and then I hear a small gasp followed by something that sets all my caveman nerves on fire. "You? What are you—"

"Millie! What's going on! Who's there with you?"

My girl doesn't respond. I hear a lot of clattering and then silence. The need to get to her overwhelms me. I call her name several more times and then instead of my beautiful girl, a man's voice says, "I'm sorry. Millie can't come to the phone right now."

The call drops. Rage like I've never felt before suffuses every cell in my body. If anything happens to her, I swear to god. I. Will. Kill. Him. Whoever he is. But I have an idea.

I bolt out of the bathroom, laser focused.

"Where are you going? You are still on the air, Doctor Dave!"

"Not anymore," I blurt out as I grab the keys to my bike and my helmet.

"But the sponsors… The station manager is on his way."

"Great, then he can do the show."

"Dave!"

I call over my shoulder, "If you want to make yourself useful, call 911 and tell them to head to Southfield Mall. A man is about to die a very painful death."

When I peel my bike out of the underground garage, the amount of ice on the road catches me off guard and forces me to slow down, despite my urgency.

I struggle to keep the bike steady at a slower speed while wrangling my phone at the same time. Shit, I've got maybe two minutes of battery power left on it.

It takes a few tries before I finally manage to hit the emergency button and reach dispatch.

"What's your emergency?"

As calmly as I can, I begin to tell the dispatcher on the phone what's happening, but then the call drops. "Fuck!" I shout, looking at my screen as the battery fully gives up the ghost.

I gun it, praying that Reagan decided to listen to me and called 911.

I don't care about the ice on the road; I don't care about anything except getting to my Millie.

I careen into the mall parking lot so hard that I lose my balance. Under normal circumstances, I could either regain my balance or set the bike down and hope for the best.

But on this ice, I'm not in control.

I set the bike down and brace myself. The bike slides out from under me, going in one direction and I go the other, tumbling and whizzing across the ice, my body crashing hard against the concrete sidewalk. I'm a little banged up, sure, but I'm feeling no pain except the pain at the thought that Millie's in trouble.

And what's my plan to get into the mall now that I'm here? I don't have one other than to crash through the locked glass automatic doors if I have to.

Chapter Eleven

Millie

It feels like all the blood in my body has pooled in my guts and I can't breathe.

Pretzel Guy is standing in front of me, looking very put out. And he's within grabbing distance.

"Who were you talking to?" he asks.

Oh god. This is bad.

Do not engage, says my brain. Also, put your hand on your stun gun without him noticing. Also, try to sound casual so you don't spook him. Also? Breathe. I finally conquer the panicky dry mouth and stammer, still not able to remember his actual name. "Hey…you? How did you get in here?"

Pretzel Guy laughs and comes closer as I inch backwards. "Well, you're a very silly girl when you get so much as a crumb of attention from a man. You really should be more careful. I watched you punch in your security code, and you didn't even try to hide it. I memorized it, waited a few minutes, then followed you inside."

I swallow, deciding not to ask him why he's here. I think it's obvious. He's a psychopath, that's why.

"Is there something you need?" I ask, trying to sound more like I'm concerned for his welfare than scared out of my wits. My hand rests on the end of my stun gun that is holstered to my belt.

Pretzel Guy stops and crosses his arms. "You know? I do need something. I need to know if you're ever going to stop playing games with me. I guess I need to take matters into my own hands. That's why, when I left work, I parked across the street and walked all the way back here in the freezing rain. Can you believe what I do for you? Every night I wait around just to say hello, just to let you flirt with me."

Not yet, Millie. Don't knock his ass down just yet. He's watching you.

"I…h-have a boyfriend," I breathe.

"Oh, Millie," he chuckles. "I think you've been misled. Whoever that was, whoever was on the phone with you? That's not your boyfriend. No suitable boyfriend would ever coerce his girl to masturbate in public."

So, he saw everything. Great. It's likely he's been watching me all night.

Then my stomach drops to the floor like I'm hurdling down the big hill on a roller coaster when I realize something. "The cameras," I whisper.

"That's right? Smart girl. I knew you were perfect for me. I've been dicking with the cameras for weeks, just to see how long it would take corporate to fix them. Turns out, they don't give a shit about you. Unlike me. It's pretty easy to see I'm the only one looking out for you. That's why I'm here. To protect you, Millie."

I try to sound breezy. "Protect me from what?"

"You don't even know my name, do you?"

"In fairness, I don't think you've ever introduced your-self. You just showed up and started talking to me in the parking lot one day. Word to the wise, don't walk up to women in parking lots. You could get yourself hurt if they don't know you're harmless."

He laughs. "You're adorable, you know that? I like a woman who talks back."

Pretzel Guy grips my upper arm with one beefy hand and pulls me away from the wall. "Come on. Let's go somewhere where we can talk."

This guy must be utterly bonkers if he thinks I'm going to let him take me to a second location, especially when the first location is a dark, abandoned shopping mall.

See, Paul? I say telepathically to my coworker. *This is what happens when you call in sick.*

"Well, actually, I need to finish checking the locks on all the doors first, and then we can go find a quiet place to talk, OK?"

His tone turns angry and he spits out, "You didn't seem too concerned about doing your job when you were fingering yourself right out here in public, did you? Not very ladylike, was it? Well, now you're with me, and I'll teach you quickly how a lady behaves…"

That word—*ladylike*—does something to me. I guess you could say I'm triggered. Everything turns several shades of red and the angry bile rises in my throat. I don't know what's going to happen next, but this? Him putting his hands on me, slut shaming me and stalking me? Not. Fucking. Tonight.

A distant clattering noise startles us both. My hand acts on its own just as Pretzel Guy's eyes flick away from me.

I point and shoot, with no plans to ask any questions later.

Chapter Twelve

David

I DO the only thing I can think to do. I pick up my bike, start it up, and position myself far enough away to reach the highest speed my bike can go. Careful not to slide on the ice this time, I barrel straight toward the accessibility ramp that leads from the parking lot, up the sidewalk, and straight toward the glass doors as fast as I can go.

Praying I don't die. Praying that this isn't the dumbest thing I've ever done in my life.

I need not have worried about the glass. The glass breaks all right. The locked metal frame, however, doesn't budge. The bike crashes into the bottom of the door frame and my body is catapulted inside the building, along with a million shards of glass.

I don't have any idea how far I fly. My body lands with a thud against the dirt inside a huge planter full of overgrown philodendrons. I roll over, groaning, and carefully remove my helmet, tossing it aside. Picking myself up, I assess any bodily damage with my eyes in the dim light because the overload of adrenaline right now means I definitely feel zero pain.

I stumble down the wide, shadowy corridor and start yelling her name. I just don't know what else to do but call out to her.

"Millie! Millie, I'm here! Where are you, baby!"

When the corridor reaches the center atrium, I see movement in the darkness to my right. I look and the first thing that registers in my brain is a figure, standing over a lump on the floor.

Panic stokes a fire in my lungs and words no longer have sound as I choke out her name.

I don't know what's going on; I barely remember who I am at this point. All I know is one thing: I have to get to her.

Chapter Thirteen

Millie

Oh my god. Doesn't one attacker in a night, like, max out the quota or something?

Pretzel Guy I can handle. He's currently passed out on the floor in front of me in a puddle of his own piss.

But now, some new, shadowy figure is barreling toward me from the east entrance of the mall.

Well, this new dude had better brace himself, because I'm pretty sure my brothers and their fellow cops and fire-fighters have busted down the doors at the west end of the mall. I can already hear the thundering of their boots and the crackling of their radios.

The cavalry is here.

For once, I don't mind having three big, overprotective brothers who sleep next to their scanners, looking out for me while I'm at work.

I can't make out this man's facial features, but his

leather jacket looks like it's been brutalized by farm equipment, and his jeans are shredded all the way down one side. He looks like he's been run over by a semi-tractor trailer and dragged fifty feet.

And he's charging toward me.

Shaking from head to toe, I aim my stun gun at the new intruder, not sure if the device has enough charge left for a second, larger attacker. "Max? Martin? Any minute now, guys…"

About ten yards away from me now, the man speaks. "Millie."

That's all it takes. I know that voice immediately. It's the voice I've been hearing in my ears every night for five years. Doctor Dave is in the fucking house. Holy shit.

He's not just a voice anymore. He's real, and he's coming toward me, and he's hurt.

"Oh my god, what happened to you?"

He doesn't answer, doesn't seem interested in the question. I can only hear him breathing heavily.

My knees tremble. And all the breath that I'd been holding in while facing Pretzel Guy, I quickly expel.

If I had any doubts about whether Doctor Dave was actually interested in me just dissipated into the air like a drop of water on a hot frying pan. In fact, everything feels hot.

"What are you doing here? You're hurt. We need to get you to the hospital!"

Still no answer. Still only a look of primal, unrelenting focus on me.

Holy shit. He's going to kiss me. He's going to kiss me hard. He's going to get blood and dirt on me and he doesn't even care. And honestly, neither do I.

He looks like Bruce Willis at the end of *Die Hard*:

wrung out, an inch from death, tired of everyone's shit, and entirely focused on getting his woman safe back in his arms.

I can't believe it. I'm going to be kissed by an action hero. Everything seems to stand still except this moment in time. He doesn't care about anything but getting to me. And I'm ready for it. I lick my lips in anticipation, my breath heaving in my chest.

But before he can reach out for me, about a dozen men and women in uniform, guns drawn, have us surrounded. My brother Max pins him the floor, his arms behind his back.

Everyone is shouting. It's pandemonium.

I struggle to shout over all the noise.

"Max! Let him go! He came here to save me from him!" I point wildly at Pretzel Guy.

My barrel-chested brother, whose knee is pressed into the doctor's spinal cord, looks up at me and grunts. "Who?"

"Him! Pretzel Guy!"

"The fuck?" Max looks confused. My brother means well, and I can't blame him for misreading the situation, what with all the chaos and echoes in this enormous, empty space.

I put my hands on my hips and everyone finally quiets down to listen to me. "Butthead. Do you realize who you are crushing with your giant Hagrid-sized leg right now? That's 'Doctor Dave,' and it looks like he busted his ass to get here because he knew I was in trouble, and I was. Now get off of him and apologize."

Max grudgingly lets him up and says he's sorry. I'm relieved to see my giant of a brother hasn't caused any further injury to my would-be rescuer.

I hear my brother mutter something about how this night has taken a turn for the weird, but I'm ignoring him now. I am purely focused on someone else: the man who made me fall for him.

Chapter Fourteen

Millie

My voice trembles in worry and wonder. "Doctor Dave? You really came here for me?"

His words tumble out dry and ragged. "I told you. It's David. For you, I'm just David. And I came here for one thing. I need those lips now if you don't mind."

My flushed face angles up to meet David halfway, but there's no need to. His lips capture mine in a searing, knee-buckling, heart-pounding kiss. Our mouths fuse together so tightly it dismantles any last thought I might have had that this is all a dream. His arms pull me close to support me as my body melts into him.

My mind so quickly closes up shop on everything else, I forget the cops are still here.

"Hey!" I hear my brother Max yell, but it's a distant echo compared to the wet, passionate smooching noises providing all the audio input I can handle.

"Dude, what the fuck do you think you're doing to my baby sister?" Martin says.

It's the "baby sister" thing that makes me finally pull away from David's kiss, even though I really, really don't want to. David grunts in displeasure and tightens his grip around me as I turn to face my brothers. "Boys, you're done here. Done babying me. Done telling me what to do. Done scaring men away. And you can run and tell Jay the same thing."

An admonished Max mutters, "Well, we're not actually done here. You still need to give us a statement about the incident."

While I do this, David keeps his arms locked around me, even under the wary gazes of my brothers.

The cavalry eventually packs it in, taking a groggy, confused Pretzel Guy away with them in handcuffs, and David and I are finally alone.

In the glow of the security lights, I examine his bruised body. "What happened to you?" I breathe. I lightly brush my fingers against David's cheekbones. His publicity photos do not do him justice. I had already formed that opinion on the day I worked security at his charity event a while ago. But up this close? He's achingly beautiful. Or maybe everything looks different, now that I know his strong jaw, sexy crow's feet, bad-boy smile, and even these bruises belong to me. The knowledge of this sends a rush through my entire body.

He shrugs. "I rode my bike here. Had to put it down on the ice. Got a little banged up. No big whoop."

My eyes flash in anger. "It's a very big whoop," I say, examining his skin while gingerly holding his face. "And very stupid of you, on this ice. Come on, the linen store is right around the corner. I know they've got first-aid kits. It's closer than the security office. I can fix you up."

He grumbles and leans his forehead against mine, a move that in movies makes me swoon. In real life, for the first time? I think my ovaries just dropped like fifteen eggs at once.

"I'd rather just go to your place and let you fix me up there," he rumbles, his breath sending a wave of warmth and tingles across my cheek.

"Sorry, John McClane, but I have to wait for my bosses to show up so I can give them the narrative of everything that happened tonight. But I'm sure we can grab one of the officers and have them dispatch an ambulance for you—"

David cuts me off in another kiss, this one tender and sweet and full of longing. His lips are soft, attentive, and caring. It nearly breaks my heart. I'm the one who should be taking care of this injured, magnificent man right now, but he won't have me fussing over him; he's made that clear. David follows the kiss with words and breaths full of trembling and an endearing neediness that tugs at all of my heartstrings. "I'm not leaving you. No matter what."

Chapter Fifteen

David

My Millie pulls me by the hand toward the towel and bedspread store, whatever the hell it's called. She unlocks the cage door and lets us both in. We quickly find the bathroom odds and ends, and sure enough, a first-aid kit.

I want to protest out of some odd macho need to present myself as tough, but my affection for this woman keeps me in check. She wants to take care of me, so I should let her.

Sitting facing each other on the end of one of the bedding displays, Millie patches me up.

First she brings me water and makes me hydrate, even though I don't feel thirsty for anything but her. I let her help me take off my motorcycle jacket and shirt, careful to avoid causing more bleeding from the shallow flesh wounds. She cleans out all the dirt and gravel that got mixed in with the ice that scraped the shit out of my arm. After she applies the peroxide to my lacerated shoulder, she blows on it. A low moan rolls out of my throat at the sensation of her breath against my bare skin.

She hears me, and her eyes meet mine with something equally primal before she checks herself. She haltingly tells me I need to take off my pants so she can finish tending to my wounds. Who am I to argue? Moments later, I'm pants-less, shirtless, and helpless against her feminine wiles. As if I ever had any hope of keeping my guard up around my Millie. The most maddening, and most boner-enhancing part of all this is that she's totally unaware she has any feminine wiles at all. Every look, every touch, from her does things to me, and she doesn't even realize it.

"You have no idea how much trouble you're in now, baby," I say.

She smirks. "I guess you'd better send me to my room to think about what I've done. Oh, wait," she says, a wicked grin radiating from her face. "Look where we are."

My gaze drops down to the bed, where her hand caresses the fluffy duvet and plumps the pillows at the strange, scaled-down headboard.

"Millie, don't play with me. I came here looking for a fight that never happened, and I'm full of pent-up testosterone. I'm so ready to spread you out, I might just do it right here on this miniature bed display."

"My bosses will be here"—she quirks her lip and checks her phone screen—"as soon as my shift ends. So, we have the time."

I exhale a ragged breath and claim her mouth, kissing her with increasing lust and urgency. My cock wants out, but not until I'm certain this is what she wants.

"Are you sure this is how you want your first time to be?"

She nods and whispers, "I need you."

"Obviously you already know there's going to be some blood.Just tell me to stop if you want me to stop."

She blushes and shakes her head. "Thanks, Doctor. But no need to worry about any of that. At least I don't think so. I popped that thing ages ago with my little vibrator."

I'm caught off guard and it must show because she laughs in between delivering sweet, sensuous kisses to my lips. So sweet and delicious, I almost forget what we're talking about.

"Are you surprised? I said I was a virgin, not a prude. I am a woman with needs, you know." She arches one flirtatious eyebrow at me.

And then the image of her touching herself, penetrating her own pussy—make that *my* pussy—with a substandard battery-operated toy instead of my dick both turns me on more than anything else in my life and makes me insanely jealous at the same time. "Holy fucking shit. You don't have any idea how sexy you are, do you?"

She shakes her head and smooths her palm down the front of her uniform shirt. "Yeah, this uniform is super alluring, I know."

I cup her chin with my hands, ignoring the sting caused by the pressure against the scrapes on the meat of my palm. "Everything about you makes me want you. It doesn't matter what you're wearing. You could be wearing a giant hot dog costume and still nothing would stand in my way of taking you to the nearest bed."

She helps me unbutton her uniform shirt and I have to stare for a moment at her partially exposed bra. "A hot dog costume? Where did that come from?" She giggles.

Shaking my head, I tell her, "I don't know. I'm amped up and not making any sense." My eyes connect with hers. "But I do know this: you're even more perfect in person. And I love that you sent me that picture of you. That you trusted me enough with it. I've been thinking of them for the past two hours. May I finally touch them?"

"Yes, of course," she whispers, reaching back and unhooking her bra, letting the cups pop loose and nearly exposing her breasts.

I slip one strap off her shoulder and kiss the skin underneath, caressing the red spot where the strap imprinted on her tender skin. I do the same with the other strap, and we let the bra and her shirt fall away. Kissing my way across her face, back to the tender spot in front of her ear, down her neck, over her collar bone, my mouth and hands meet up at the crest of the two most beautiful mounds on earth.

My Millie moans quietly as I smooth my hand over the nipples, one way and then the other, until they are fully pebbled under my touch and ready to be teased.

She sucks in a breath as my tongue traces circles around the taut, rosy buds. My kisses deepen and her breathing shallows.

"Lie on your back and let me kiss you all over."

"All…all over?" she asks, her voice breathy.

I trace my fingers slowly from her nipples, down her stomach until I reach the button of her uniform pants. Snapping the button open, I flatten my palm against her skin and slide my hand down between the elastic of her panties and her skin.

A soft moan escapes her.

"All. Over," I tell her.

My lips graze the supple skin between her breasts. Her fingernails lightly scraping over the areas of my uninjured skin feels like a brush with heaven.

The hand inside her panties slides lower and lower until my fingers find the warmth of her split.

My fingers slide between her folds, warming in her

juices. My cock grows another two inches knowing how much honey she's made for me. "Oh, baby, if you could only know what it means to have you so wet for me."

My mouth lands somewhere below her navel and I feel her body softly jerk. I murmur sweet and dirty words against the soft skin of her lower belly, punctuating my words with small reassuring kisses. "My girl. My good girl with the sweet, juicy pussy. That pussy belongs to me. All for me and nobody else." When her breath calms, she tugs off her pants for me.

"All for you, David."

I growl and kiss my way lower and lower, reveling in the sounds of her voice and her breath catching.

Millie's fingertips scrape across my scalp, sending tingles through me so intense I have to work to remain focused. "After the first time I ever heard your voice, I bought my first vibrator. Almost every morning after work, before I go to sleep, the memory of your voice gives me an orgasm."

I'm so floored, I nearly fall right off the tiny little bed. To process what she's told me, I pause what I'm doing, but probably take a minute too long, because I can see on Millie's sweet, innocent face that she thinks I'm having second thoughts. No way can I allow her to think that. I come back up to face level and devour her mouth again, pulling her close to me and whispering in her ear. "I'm just a man, and I'm real, and I'm not going anywhere if you'll let me stay with you."

Her delicate fingers playing against my chest and abs nearly send me off a cliff of pleasure, and I have to grit my teeth and growl to hold myself together.

"David. I need you. Now." Her hand is dangerously close to my cock, and my cock is desperate for some touch.

"You want to touch it? See it? Go ahead and take it out. It's large for you, sweetheart."

Her breath hitches and she pulls it out. I help by tugging down my boxer briefs. My cock springs free with a heavy whap against my abdomen.

"Oh!" she gasps before her mouth spreads into a wide, wicked smile. I look down between us and see her fingers hovering over it. "Wow."

"Touch it. Play with it. Slap it. Don't be scared; it's just a dick."

"It's so…red. And it keeps moving when I talk. Does it hurt?"

I laugh and kiss her with my tongue. "It likes the sound of your voice. Nah, it doesn't hurt. It just really, really wants inside you now."

Her hand grips my shaft, and I suck in a huge breath. God, she's delicate and firm at the same time. All this time, her touch is exactly what I've been missing. My cock is so happy I have to control my urge to thrust mightily into her two hands that circle it.

"Fuck," I groan. "Dammit. I don't have a condom. Sorry, baby, I can honestly say I wasn't expecting tonight to go like this. It's OK. Stay still and let me pleasure you."

She only moans out my name but I don't hear the rest as I paint a wet trail of kisses down her chest, over her tummy and finally land my mouth between her legs.

Her hips arc upward abruptly, as if she was not expecting this move.

My thumbs slowly spread open her folds; her gleaming pink wetness provokes me to praise any and all deities above or below who may have taken part in creating this unbelievably sexy woman. I take her heat like I'm dying of thirst, her sweet slickness trembling and dripping with every kiss, every moan, every lick. I let her juices fill me, heal me, obliterating any memory of ever tasting another.

"Sweetheart, hold on to something. I'm gonna suck your clit into my mouth."

I glance upward and she throws her head back, her teeth biting down on one full, rosy lip. Her fingers latch into the fake brass miniature headboard. I follow through on my promise and gently suck her clit into my mouth with a deep tonguing kiss. My sweet Millie's hips launch into me. She's crying out, wriggling and moaning in pleasure. My mouth fully lavishes her clit with the attention it deserves, bathing it with my tongue and sucking it into my mouth over and over again with heavy, loud, sucking noises. She tastes like heaven and I can't get enough.

Millie's hips rise up off the duvet again, and I take the opportunity to hold her with both arms and pull her hips as tight to me as I can.

As far as I'm concerned, no reason exists why her body should not be fused into mine, at any time of day or night. I don't need water, or food, or sunlight. I just need her.

When I feel she's close to coming, I slip one finger inside her pussy, gently stretching. Her moans and pants increase.

"More," she breathes.

Two fingers enter, stretching her out for my cock.

My probing fingers and my mouth on her clit is finally too much. She shouts my name through a bone-rattling orgasm while her body clenches down on my fingers. I rise up and hold her tight against my body, steadying her while wave after wave hits her, spasming around my two fingers still deep inside her.

I rumble against the soft skin of her neck. "Do you want to know what you taste like?"

"Yes," she half whispers.

I slowly slip my fingers out of her and hold her face with that hand. "C'mere," I whisper, bringing her lips to mine and sharing her sweet sticky juices with her.

Millie sweetly moans through the kiss.

Everything about this woman in my arms feels like the sweetest, most pure thing I've ever been privileged to hold, and I'm never letting her go. Even her greedy little grabby hands, now pulling me by the cock to encourage me to settle between her thighs, are pure. She's untouched, unrehearsed, unschooled. Unbelievably sexy.

I laugh into her shoulder, which sends another aftershock through her. "I told you I don't have a condom, so I'll have to pull out, OK, baby?"

"Oh," she says, undaunted. "Here."

To my surprise, she pulls a condom from the tiny pocketbook within the pocket of her discarded uniform pants.

"I'm dead curious why you're walking around with a condom in your pocket," I tease her.

"I have three single brothers. I borrow from them all the time. I figured if I wanted some D, I'd better be prepared to welcome that abundance into my life. You know, like in *The Secret*."

We laugh and together sheathe my cock in protection.

We're still laughing even as I slide my length into her, inch by inch, until she's ready for my fullness.

"All the way, baby. Please," she begs.

The teasing and the laughter gradually subside with every gentle push. Our giggles and grins are soon replaced with what I can only describe as passion, wonder and a sense of overwhelming joy.

Once she's comfortable with my movements, I feel her legs wrap around me, her feet interlocking behind my back, spreading her wider for me.

"I can't get enough. I just can't get deep enough. I want more of you. I want to feel all of you."

Millie reaches for me, and we share a kiss that makes my heart explode. The way we rock together, mussing all the overpriced blankets and pillows on this ridiculous display, compels brand new urges in me. My mouth has a tendency to get me in trouble, but now I just have to let it out.

"I've never said this to anybody before but…I love you."

Her thighs squeeze my middle. Her eyes go round in shock. "You what? You love me?"

I push into her with a slightly rougher thrust. "I'll say it as many times as you want me to. I love you, Millie. And next time we do this, there's not going to be any condoms. Especially not one you stole from your brother's night table. You got that? I don't want to do radio anymore. I just want to do life with you and I want to start as soon as possible. Tell me you can handle that."

A tiny tear sparkles in the corner of her eye. She doesn't need to say anything. I know she's feeling the same thing I'm feeling. Our unearthly connection can't be denied.

"I love you too," she whispers, slamming her body in tighter to me, gripping me closer, taking me even deeper than I thought possible. Her nails scraping my shoulder blades, combined with her kisses on my neck, finally send me over the edge. I release a growl against her breast as I explode inside her, reveling in our joined bodies.

We hold each other close until the surging subsides, and then keep holding on to each other, both of us over-whelmed and overjoyed by this new thing that has fallen over us both like a huge, soft, warm blanket.

I spoil her face with small kisses all over. "Baby, what

are we gonna do with this duvet? We messed it up pretty badly," she says.

I shrug. "Take it home as a souvenir?"

She giggles. "Might as well. Pretty sure I'm fired, anyway."

I don't want to stop kissing her, but she's right. We should probably clean up after ourselves before her bosses get here. And pay for whatever can't be salvaged.

I smile playfully as I slowly slide my spent cock from her warmth. "Now, if only I knew where to find a towel to get us both cleaned up, we can take that with us, too."

Epilogue 1

Eight Months Later

Millie

The nice thing about my husband being a former radio celebrity is we can usually maintain relative anonymity while out in public. That is, until someone at a nearby table hears my husband speak, then all bets are off.

"Excuse me, I couldn't help overhearing your incredibly sexy voice from where I was sitting, and I just have to say I miss you on the radio so much. When are you coming back? Would you mind posing for a selfie?"

The random bombshell already has her camera poised and ready, and is leaning her torso toward my husband in a way that can only be described as a blatantly rehearsed, not-so-innocent boob graze.

When I first became swept up in this whirlwind romance eight months ago, I might have felt like I was on shaky ground at times. David and I stole our kisses, intimate moments, and private conversations in between calls from corporate media lawyers threatening to sue him over breach of contract. David's abrupt exit from the airwaves also caused him to be very much in demand for a short time by local media outlets seeking interviews and explanations.

He's continued to be Doctor Dave in the eyes of everyone in town, but he's proven to me time and time again he was simply David Hart, M.D. *My* David.

The ring on my finger and my ever-expanding pregnant belly serve as convenient outward signals to anyone still hoping for a shot at the city's former most eligible bachelor. At least, most people got the hint. Boob Graze, however…

"That's very kind of you to say, but I actually do mind. As you can see," David says, breaking eye contact with our visitor to nod in my direction and give me a tender look that still makes my knees quiver under the table, even at seven months pregnant. "I'm having dinner with my wife."

The stranger stands upright, looking shocked at having been rebuffed. She can't help herself from looking me up and down with a withering glance.

I grin at her as I spin a huge ball of pasta onto my fork. "He just doesn't have time for radio anymore, what with these pregnancy hormones demanding all the various forms of sexual congress multiple times a day. He is quite the soldier. Bless him," I say.

The woman narrows her eyes in revulsion as I stuff the contents of my fork into my mouth and roll my eyes back in my head in pure pleasure. It's not acting; I crave pasta and Alfredo sauce like the dickens these days.

When she finally gets the hint and stalks away in a snit,

I notice David's papa bear crawling its way up out of its cave. He doesn't like the way some of his fans treat me.

Everyone in town is still talking about the virgin who brought down Doctor Dave. David, as I call my husband, gets pretty riled up when the local news paints me as a pariah who destroyed the career of a beloved radio personality.

As for me, I'm oddly satisfied with my notoriety.

One gentle hand on his arm stays the angry beast, and David settles. Our eyes lock and his breathing evens out.

He's about to ask for to-go boxes for the rest of our dinner, as well as my dessert, so we can get the hell out of Dodge, but I stop him.

"David, it doesn't bother me what anyone says. I've been called quiet, unassuming, reclusive and even boring. So if everyone wants to believe my pussy has the power to destroy, I find it amusing. Maybe even a little bit exhilarating," I add with a sassy shoulder shimmy.

"This protective streak isn't going to go away any time soon," he says. "Sorry, but it's gonna get even worse when the baby arrives. And now, all I want to do is go home and eat that tiramisu off the town pariah's tits."

I pout. "But then what will I eat?"

"I've got at least one real big cannoli for that mouth of yours."

I gasp as warmth pools inside my body and threatens to drench my maternity undies. His commanding dirty talk always works for me. And lately, he only has to provide some mild innuendo for me to be good to go.

"You're going to make your seven-months-pregnant wife get on her knees? Because I definitely won't be able to reach the Big D from the passenger seat," I say with a pout, knowing that he does not mean for me to do either of those things.

My increasingly aroused husband does his best not to exceed the speed limit to get me home. Soon enough, we're in our cozy king-sized bed, a bed outfitted, of course, with the same bedding we ruined at the linen store display. We barely make it through the door when David sweeps me into his arms as if I haven't gained thirty-five pounds of baby weight since the first time he'd carried me to bed.

And now as I lie on my side, he expertly spoils me with a lower back massage that sends happy tingles rippling across every inch of my skin. When he moves on to working over the muscles in my ass, I bite back a moan.

He notices this and leans in close to whisper in my ear. "Let it out, baby. I love it when you free yourself."

I'm so aroused that when his hand parts my thighs from behind to massage my wet folds, my entire body shudders as I moan and squirt my arousal.

"Fuck, baby. You're soaked. Only one thing to do with all this juice covering my hand." His wicked whispers in my ear combined with the sound of his hand coating his cock with my sticky essence nearly has me coming immediately.

Something dark and hormonal, primal and bossy rises up inside me. Panting, I order my husband to lie on his back.

He groans softly. "I know what you're thinking, baby. No way you're not going first. Not in my bed. I always take care of you."

I sigh. "But hormones won't be satisfied. You're not going to deny your pregnant wife her little snack, are you? Besides, I need to remind you who that D belongs to."

"Baby, you're not jealous of that silly woman from the restaurant, are you?"

My "no" comes out a little too forcefully. He is not convinced.

He chuckles while he nuzzles my ear. My husband has a way of making me reach my release just by doing that. But I know what he's up to and suddenly my inner domme is not having it. Through gritted teeth, I get real bossy. "Assume the position, David, I'm gonna show you what's mine."

David growls roughly into my neck, spreading goose flesh everywhere. "Fuck, baby. Not fair." He finally rests his back against the head rest, his legs spread out to cradle me as I nestle myself between his thighs. Still lying on my most comfortable side, I rest my head against his pelvic bone so I'm eye level with his huge, throbbing, glistening cock.

I gently tilt his shaft toward my mouth, then slip the tip of him between my lips, licking off the pearly bead of precum.

"You taste yourself on me, Millie? You taste that gorgeous pussy on my skin?"

I moan and take him in deeper into my mouth, my body flooding with pleasure at making him feel owned by me.

His words incite a fire so hot, and combined with our flavors mixed together, I barely need any stimulation at all to come.

A year ago I never would have thought I'd eagerly take a man's cock in my mouth, let alone be this bold about it. Or about sex in general. A year ago, I was an unsatisfied virgin looking anywhere for advice. But David gave me something far better than advice, or even better than sex.

Everything about this man speaks to everything in me, And not just his radio voice.

It's his real voice, his mind, his soul, whispering directly into mine, and mine into his.

<h1 style="text-align:center">Epilogue 2</h1>

Five Years Later

DAVID

I CAN TELL the energy of the house is wonky as soon as I start downstairs after recording my podcast.

Soundproofing a portion of the finished attic space to create a makeshift studio wasn't my choice; I'd rather be accessible at all times in case Millie or our daughter Emily needs me. But a few years back, Millie could tell I was missing something, apart from my day-to-day work as a doctor and my volunteer work at the free clinic. She could tell I missed speaking into a mic, offering advice, interacting with an audience. So, she encouraged me to start a relationship-and-parenting advice podcast. And she insisted on the soundproofing to make it as professional as possible.

On this night, the night before our daughter's fifth

birthday, Emily is sound asleep, so I'm trying to be quiet as I head down the creaky wooden staircase of our house. Doesn't much matter how hard I try to be silent as a ninja, though, judging from the racket coming from the kitchen.

"Ugh!" The frustrated scream stops me in my tracks for half a second at the bottom of the stairs. If I valued my life, I would turn tail and run the other way when I hear my wife's frustrated exclamations coming from the kitchen.

But I'm Doctor friggin' Dave. I run toward danger, even if that danger comes in the form of last-minute party-prep panic.

"Millie. Baby." I speak calmly and haltingly from the kitchen doorway, careful not to provoke the exasperated mama bear any further. Studying her from behind, I see my wife and the mother of my child has somehow gotten white icing in her messy bun.

The typical male part of me wants to ask whether she has icing spilled on other parts of her and whether she requires my assistance in cleaning it off. But I would not be Doctor Dave if I didn't know how to read an audience. I can tell this is not the time for my filthy suggestions.

"How can I help?" I ask.

It's then that I see her shoulders shudder and her hands grip the table to prop herself up. She's staring down at a quite messy but still delicious-looking three-tiered birthday cake.

Through sobs, Millie blurts out, "You can go back in time and marry someone who actually knows what she's doing at this motherhood thing!"

One thing I can't stand is when Millie is hard on herself. Nope. Not having it. In an instant I'm wrapped around her, letting her cry it out all over me. She's still holding a messy spatula in one hand as icing and tears are probably making a sticky mess on my t-shirt. But I don't care about the mess. All I want is to make it better.

"Oh. OK. Well in that case, do you think the random lady who once slipped her hand down my pants would do a better job at making a homemade cake? Or, decorating the party room with a hundred pink balloons and tissue paper flowers?" I ask, gesturing at the explosion of pastel in the living room adjacent to the kitchen.

She breathes out a small watery laugh against my shoulder. "No, she'd probably have spent all your money by now."

I smile and gently pet her hair, then lick off the icing that transferred onto my hand. "You're right; no money left to raise babies, let alone buy decorations. What about Boob Graze Lady? You think she'd make a better wife and mommy?"

Millie shudders against me, but this time, it's in laughter. I exhale in relief; she's coming around. "Nah," she says, using my shirt to dab at her eyes before looking up at me. "The way she was watching me eat, she probably doesn't allow for birthday cake. She probably lets her kids eat carrots as a high carb treat on special days."

There's my girl. I give her a squeeze. I look over at the cake. "Baby, I think it looks fine. It's midnight. Why don't you leave that for the morning and come to bed?"

The truth is, the cake looks like an absolute mess, and it doesn't matter.

I just wish my amazing wife knew that.

Her shoulders droop and she looks disappointed in herself. "The coriander lime buttercream doesn't taste like coriander or lime. It just tastes like vanilla!"

Whoa, I think. "I don't have any idea what you just said but vanilla sounds just fine for a kid's party."

She huffs. "But you don't understand. When I asked

her what flavor she wanted, she said 'the beach,' so I was going for a tropical theme. But the coconut flavor doesn't even come through in the cake, the icing is a disaster, and the fondant palm tree looks like a green turd. The Mom Squad and all their kids will be here in twelve hours and that's not enough time to fix this cake, make the appetizers, assemble the party favors, fill the piñata and also shower and sleep."

I nod and smile while she goes on. Meanwhile, I surreptitiously taste a part of the cake that's fallen down. I don't know anything about fancy baking, but I do enjoy food, and this cake is hands down her best cake yet. Because of course it is. Because my sweet Millie has made homemade cakes for my birthday and Emily's birthday every year.

Just like knitting or tasing bad guys, my Millie can do anything she sets her mind to. Molding fondant to look like a palm tree, however, not so much. She's right. It does look like a green turd.

"Millie, look at me," I say, cupping her face. "This cake is amazing. Emily doesn't know what the beach tastes like and none of her little friends are going to care that the lime and coconut and cumin—"

"Coriander," she corrects.

"Yes, that. None of them are going to ask what happened to the intended flavor profile. So, that leaves the other parents. Is this cake for them, or for Emily?"

Millie smiles sweetly at the thought of our bright-eyed, freckled free spirit, fast asleep upstairs. I'm biased, but I've never seen anyone so full of so much love for a child that she radiates with it. Millie closes her eyes for a moment. I can tell she's bursting with happiness combined with sadness that our baby is turning five. She expresses her love so freely it almost hurts my heart to witness it.

I softly trace the pad of my thumb over one of her closed eyes, feeling her lashes brush against my skin. "Ask yourself how much you actually care what the Mom Squad thinks," I suggest.

Saying the phrase "Mom Squad" out loud makes me cringe. Mostly good people, but corny name. The Mom Squad refers to the local parenting group that Millie found online, back when she first started seeking out the company of other moms in the area. Even though I've cut back on my hours treating patients to make sure I'm present as much as possible to help out, I could see early on that Millie was going to need extra support. She can be a bit of a hermit if left to her own devices. I don't mind—I love having my girls all to myself—but the friends she's made in the group have given us both lots of help. A few of them have even made appearances on the podcast to talk about everything from breastfeeding to sex after childbirth.

"Not at all. Except for Valerie. And Jenny. And Tara. They're cool," she replies.

I agree. "See? And none of the little hooligans are gonna care. They're just going to be grateful for cake and games and entertainment."

Her eyes go wide. "Oh no. Babe, did you talk to Max about all that?"

Brushing my thumbs against her cheekbones, I place a kiss on the end of her nose. "Your brother is on board, and he'll be here."

She bites her lip, looking skeptical. "And you told him about the ruffled pirate shirt?"

I didn't, but he'll wear it. Her big lug of a brother will show up and wear the damn pirate shirt and like it, if it means making my Emily and Millie happy. "Yes," I lie.

Millie squints at me. "Don't lie."

"Listen," I say. "He will do it if he ever wants a chance

at asking out Val." The one single mother in the Mom Squad got Max's attention when I talked to her on the show about raising a baby on her own after her boyfriend flaked. Max has been bugging us for her phone number ever since.

Millie grins up at me wickedly. "You're a bigger manipulator than anyone in the Mom Squad."

I raise one shoulder in acknowledgment, now forgetting what we were talking about because for some reason my hand has traveled down to her shoulder and has sneakily tugged apart the V neck of her nightshirt. My focus is now entirely on the icing smudge on her sternum.

She sees the dark look in my eye and laughs. I pull the fabric away some more, stretching out her shirt, and taking my other hand away from her face to cinch my arm around her waist.

"What are you doing, Doctor?"

A growl escapes me when I attack the icing on her chest, filling my mouth with the taste of vanilla and a hint of citrus. I run my tongue over the sweetness, licking up every drop.

"Prepping for a full physical exam," I say.

Millie squirms in my arms, her voice squeaking out one last weak protest. "But...the cake."

"It's fine," I grunt, sliding my hand down to grasp a handful of her ass. Her sweetness, her hard work, her sharp mind, and her luscious body still make my cock rigid as hell at the slightest provocation after five-plus years together.

I pull her into me and grind my body against hers in some kind of primal need to show her what she does to me. I share the taste of the icing with her, my tongue teasing its way into her sweet mouth.

She relaxes in my arms.

"David," she whispers, returning grind for grind. "You're making me wet."

I quirk my lip. "Then we'd better go upstairs and walk the plank."

Millie traces the tip of her tongue across my bottom lip while her hand lets go of the spatula. It clatters to the floor. I suck in my breath when that hand finds its way down to cup my balls.

With her saucy mouth a hair's breadth away from my lips, she responds, "OK, but you gotta promise to let me taste your coconuts first." She leans back to meet my gaze, her eyes full of the fire that I love so much. In fact, I love it more and more every day that we spend together.

I don't know whether to laugh or spread her out on the kitchen table immediately, right here next to the cake. She can taste my coconuts anytime she wants to.

In fact, Millie can have me any way she wants to, whether she makes homemade cakes, orders store-bought cakes, does it all herself, or hires a nanny. I don't care how she wants to live her life, as long as she does what makes her happy and she sees the same amazing person in herself that I see every morning lying next to me in my bed.

As long as she's mine, and she's my Millie. Forever.

THE END

Thank you for reading Doctor Dave! If you enjoyed this title, read Officer Max next to get Millie's brother Max's happily ever after.

Also by Abby Knox

All my books are stand-alone romances, each with its own HEA.
No cliffhangers or cheating!

My latest releases:

Reckless Royals

Favored Prince (Torben and Hailey)

Bad Prince (Etienne and Kala)

Wild Prince (Sigurd and Stasi)

Forgotten Prince (Jakob and Jo)

Stolen Crown (May 2024)

Love Games series

Roll For Initiative

Roll for Damage

Roll for Charisma

Roadside Attractions series:

Roadside Attraction (insta love)

Claiming Fate (rivals to lovers)

Falling into Fate (long lost friends to lovers)

Fate's Dark Shadows (age gap)

Rode Hard (insta love, dating app)

Crash into Me (grumpy mountain man)

Snowed Under (second chance, later-in-life)

Wish List (holiday, older heroine/younger hero)

Fate's Holi-Date (he falls first, age gap)

Wood Brothers series

(OTT alpha insta-love. Set in the same universe as Roadside Attractions)

Nailed

Screwed

Drilled

Small-Town Gossip

(Set in Darling Creek, Montana. Tropes include: small town, insta love, workplace romance)

Do That To Me

Say That To Me

Love That For Me

The Mail-Order Brides of Darling Creek

(tropes include: age gap, mail/e-mail order brides, small town, insta love, cowboy)

A Baby for the Bride

A Week to Wed

Her Guardian Groom

The Cowboy Auction of Darling Creek

(tropes include: dating auction, small town, cowboy, insta love)

The Cowgirl's Bid

Winning the Cowboy

Her Forbidden Prize

Paradise Passions

(vacation romances)

Babymoon

Honeymoon Hideout

Need more stand alones? I've got plenty…

Are You For Reel?

The Bodyguard and His Bunny

A Little Amusement

511 Kissme Lane

V-Card Vacation

Hail Mary

Additional titles are available on iBooks, Barnes & Noble, Everand, Smashwords, Fable, and on my website at authorabbyknox.com

Happy reading!

About the Author

Abby Knox writes feel-good, high-heat romance that readers have described as quirky, sexy, adorable, and hilarious.

Abby's favorite tropes include: Forced proximity, opposites attract, grumpy/sunshine, age gap, boss/employee, fated mates/insta-love, and more. Abby is heavily influenced by Buffy the Vampire Slayer, Gilmore Girls, and LOST. But don't worry, she won't ever make you suffer like Luke & Lorelai.

Say hello at authorabbyknox@gmail.com, or visit www.authorabbyknox.com for more information. While you're there, don't forget to sign up for Abby's newsletter to keep up with her latest releases and access bonus materials!